CHANGING

❧

A MEDITATION JOURNAL FOR YOUNG ADULTS

BY
LINDA A. MEYER, PH.D.

Recovery Communications, Inc.
P.O. Box 19910 • Baltimore, MD 21211 • (410) 243-8558

DEDICATION

To Phyllis and Chrissy, the two people who have taught me and continue to teach me the most about recovery. Thank you.

and

To Sara and Josh, the teens I know best. May you continue to prosper. I am so very glad you came to our family to stay.

and

To Lilly and Matt, the young adults I am getting to know. I am very proud of you both.

The information printed herein is not intended to be considered counseling or other professional advice by the publisher, author, or contributors.

Copyright © 1997 by Linda Meyer
Printed in the United States of America
International Standard Book Number 0-9615995-6-1
Library of Congress Catalog Card Number 97-076520

Acknowledgments

I learned almost everything in this book from other people too numerous to mention, and somehow integrated it so that I no longer can recall what I really learned when or from whom.

I am grateful for the privilege of working with each of my clients. Each of them teaches me.

I was very fortunate to begin working 30 years ago with Siegfried Engelmann, because he taught me how to think about curriculum as well as how to allocate time for working and engage in our task — sit down, grind something out, and always end up with more at the end of each day than we had when we started, even if we had wadded up and pitched many pages. Later, it was Wes Becker who began to teach me to think about every word.

I am also grateful that my husband, Don Pilcher, supports me morning, noon, and night as I write and talk about what I am writing.

This is a book about me and how I grow and change. Before I begin my book, I will draw a picture of myself here.

I am _Madison Stech1_
This is my book.

Introduction

Go through this book in the order in which you find it, except for the entries entitled "Holidays." Do those around Thanksgiving and other major holidays that you celebrate. The last entry is entitled "My Birthday." Read it on your birthday.

Today is _____

Choices

As I think about what I want to do with my life, I know that I have many choices ahead of me. What kind of person do I want to become? What kind of grades will I get? How much do I choose to study? What kinds of friends will I pick? How do I want to spend my spare time? Perhaps most important, how will I make my choices?

Answer this: "How will I make my choices?"

or draw a picture of yourself making a choice, or the choice you want most to make.

Today is _____

Self-Care

From the time I was ten or eleven years of age, there have been a lot of ways that I can take care of myself. I can list some ways that I can take care of myself — talking about feelings, studying, playing, brushing my teeth, bathing, resting, exercising, walking away from someone who is being unkind to me, washing my hair, and eating well-balanced meals.

The challenge is to pick the ways to take care of myself at any given time. Sometimes I need one thing, and sometimes I need something quite different.

Write or draw a picture about how to take care of yourself best right now.

Today is _____

Family Systems

A family is a system. This means that every member of a family has an influence on every other member of that family. What affects one, affects all.

In healthy families, the members can talk about problems, trust each other to work together for solutions, and express their feelings, whatever those feelings may be. In unhealthy families, a very different process takes over.

In unhealthy families, members often take roles that work together to protect the family, especially if it is a family that does not talk, trust, or allow expression of feelings. Members of such families slide into roles because of their pain. These roles become their walls of defense, their ways of taking care of themselves in the midst of their problems.

Behind the walls of defense, each member of the family has powerful feelings much like the feelings of everyone else in the family.

Think about your family. Now think of a problem that has happened in your family. Did you talk about it and know that you could trust each other?

Was each member of your family free to express his or her feelings?

What feelings did you have around this problem? Can you draw or write what that felt like?

Today is _____

FEELINGS

Recognizing and expressing feelings is an important part of taking care of myself. Yet sometimes I have trouble getting my feelings out, or even figuring out what they are. When I have this problem, I can sit quietly and "listen" to my body.

When I am having painful feelings, if I sit very quietly for several seconds, I can often feel where the pain is trapped in my body. Once I know this, I can begin to do things to release my feelings.

Sit very still. Listen. What do you hear?

What are some other things you do to help you name and release feelings?

Today is _____

SOLVING PROBLEMS

Whenever I have a problem, the first thing I need to do is STOP. Then I need to CALM DOWN in order to be able to THINK about what to do before I act. If I STOP and CALM DOWN and THINK, I am much more likely to make a good choice about how to act.

Some things I can do to help me CALM DOWN include slow, easy breathing, imagining myself in a peaceful scene, and listening to gentle music.

What are some ways you use to help yourself CALM DOWN?

What problems are you facing now? STOP, CALM DOWN, and THINK. As you stop, calm down, and think, what thoughts come to you? What are you thinking about right now?

Today is _____

Family Roles: THE HERO

Counselors who have worked with troubled families realize that kids in such families often take on roles, just like actors in a play. These roles have names. One such role a family member may slide into is that of the Hero. A Hero is easy to recognize. This is the person who does everything "right."

The family Hero looks good. In fact, the Hero looks so good that he or she gives the impression that nothing could be wrong with their family — just see how good they look! This person probably gets very good grades, keeps a neat room, dresses in outfits that always match, is good at whatever sports they try, is always volunteering and trying to "make a difference," works long hours, and takes care of a lot of others.

Family Heroes look good. Who are the Heroes or likely Heroes that you know? Make a list of them below. Then, next to their names, write a line or two about why you think they are Heroes.

Today is _____

Family Roles: THE HERO

It is important for me to remember that the Hero role is just that, a role. By this, I mean that I am only seeing the way a family member is behaving. Such a person is playing a role in the family, just as they might have a role in a play or a TV show or a movie.

It is very important for me to remember that a person playing Superman, for example, is not Superman — he is playing Superman. A person who acts like Wonder Woman is only playing Wonder Woman — a Hero role. It is the same in a family. One person can take the Hero role and play the Hero. But that does not really mean that the person is the Hero.

Write about the Heroes you know. How do you think they have tried to make everyone and everything "look good"?

Today is _____

Family Roles:
THE TROUBLEMAKER/SCAPEGOAT

Another role that a person may play in a troubled family is called the Troublemaker/Scapegoat. This is the person that other family members tend to point their fingers at as "The Problem." This may be the child who has temper tantrums, or the one who steals things at the corner grocery, or the one who experiments with alcohol or other drugs. In general, this person is often thought of as a troublemaker.

Yet the Scapegoat is playing a role, just like the Hero. It is important for me to remember that the Troublemaker/Scapegoat role is just that — a role. In fact, once there is a Hero in the family, it is highly likely that someone else will slide into the Troublemaker/Scapegoat role. When the Hero role is already filled, a family member tends to move into another role. It just happens. It is not something that anyone plans.

Think about people you know who have been or are the Troublemaker/Scapegoats in their families. What have those people done? Who has pointed fingers at them?

Today is _____

Family Roles:
THE TROUBLEMAKER/SCAPEGOAT

It is hard for me to recognize that a Hero and a Scapegoat have anything in common. But as I learn more about roles, I begin to understand that Heroes and Scapegoats actually do have a lot in common. The most important thing they have in common is that both Heroes and Scapegoats are playing roles.

Why have they slid into these roles? Family members slide into roles when they are in pain. They slide into roles when there are difficult, painful things going on that they are not talking about.

It is also the case that in these families people cannot trust each other and are unable to show their feelings. Now, whenever I see someone in a role, I can look past that role and realize that it is just a defense. People take on these defenses to protect themselves from what they are really feeling.

Think about Scapegoats and Heroes that you know. In one column, write down what they are doing in their roles. Next to that column, write down what you think each one's defense is.

Today is _____

Family Roles:
THE MASCOT

Another role that family members often take on is the role of the Mascot. A Mascot is the family jokester. This may be the person who becomes the class clown in school. This person might also keep the family laughing by saying funny things or doing cute things that draw attention away from their pain. Frequently this is the person who likes to tell jokes and make light of things that are going on.

Lots of Mascots fool people by acting like they do not have a care in the world. But I can see that Mascots act that way as a defense, just as the Hero and the Scapegoat have defenses. I can see that the Mascot's defense is humor, just as the Hero's defense is behaving as if everything is fine and the Scapegoat's defense is getting into trouble and drawing attention away from unpleasant things going on in the family.

Do you know anyone who is a Mascot? Think back about kids you have known in school. List the names of kids who have been the class clowns. Think about the things they did. Do you now think that these kids may have been their family's Mascots? How were these kids treated in school?

Today is _____

Family Roles:
THE MASCOT

When I think about a Hero, a Scapegoat, and a Mascot, I realize that they all have defenses that draw attention away from what is going on in the family. The Hero draws attention by getting into perfectionism — this makes everything look just fine. Most people will look at a Hero and think, "How could anything be wrong in that family? That child is so perfect!"

The Scapegoat draws attention away from the total family, too, because people look at the Scapegoat and wonder, "What is the matter with him/her?" Most people do not look past the Scapegoat to wonder what is going on with the rest of the family. The Mascot draws a lot of attention away from the family, too, by keeping everyone laughing, and while everyone is laughing they cannot (or do not) look at the family as it really is. I must remember that each of these is a role, a defense that the person has gone into, because of problems.

Write below about a family that you know. Put down the Mom and the Dad. Then list the kids (you can make up names, or just put "older boy," "youngest girl," etc. — just so that you know who you are writing about) and then identify their roles. How are the family members that you list taking care of themselves?

Today is _____

Family Roles:
THE LONELY/LOST CHILD

Another role a family member may slide into is that of the Lonely/Lost Child. The Lonely/Lost Child is often the family member who gets the least attention. This child can get less attention than the other children because, instead of doing things that draw attention to himself or herself, this person withdraws from the family, often into a world of his or her own. It is as if they become invisible. In this way, they may truly be lost.

This is the person who seldom talks, who may watch TV or read a lot or wear a headset in order to create a little private world. Lost Children seldom attract attention to themselves. These children do not cause problems in school. In fact, these may be the children who get overlooked in families as well as in school. These are the children who seem to fade into the woodwork.

Do you know any Lonely/Lost Children? How do the Lost Children that you know behave? Draw a picture of how their faces look to you.

Today is _____

Outsides and Insides

The last few weeks, as I have been reading and thinking about roles, it would be easy for me to think about people as really being the way they are in their roles. In other words, I could think of the Scapegoat as really a defiant, angry person. I could also think of the Mascot as an active, entertaining person who likes to make others laugh.

Because it is easy for me to fall into this trap, it is very important for me to remember always that these are just the roles that these people are playing. When I look at the roles that people are in, I am only looking at their behavior. Their behavior shows me the roles that they are in, but it does not in any way show me what is really going on inside them.

When you look at someone playing a Scapegoat, what are that person's behaviors? What are the behaviors of a Hero, a Mascot, and a Lost Child? Make a list of each.

Today is _____

DENIAL

Today as I start this reading, I can see that I slipped into a role because of problems in my family, but perhaps those problems do not really affect me much. In fact, I am thinking that I really do not have many feelings behind the wall of defenses I built with the behaviors in my role.

I wonder if what I am going through at this point is what I have heard others talk about as "denial." I have even heard one of my friends say, "Denial is not just a river in Egypt!" Until today, I wondered what this meant. Today I think I may know. Maybe my supposing that I do not have feelings behind my wall of defenses is really a part of denial. Am I denying how I really feel?

Write about what you think denial is.

Now draw a picture of how you feel when you are denying something.

Today is _____

DENIAL

I am beginning to wonder if other people in my family also deny the reality of what is going on. As I look around, I see that some of them either seem to ignore things that have happened or else really play them down. What I especially notice is that some of my family members seem to deny their feelings. They seem to need to stay in their roles. I wonder what is going on here.

When I stand back, I can see we have had many problems. I can see we have often ignored pretty important things, things that I now realize are big deals. To pretend they are unimportant, or to pretend they did not happen, is also a type of denial.

What sorts of things do you think have been ignored in your family?

What do you think would be a better way to handle those things today?

Today is _____

Pacing Myself

A way of taking care of myself is learning to take breaks when I feel that I need them, and learning to juggle more than one thing at a time. This is part of learning how to pace myself. If I let myself work on just one thing at a time, the chances are good that I may feel my feelings move through highs and lows as I move through whatever I am working on. Here is a drawing of what that looks like.

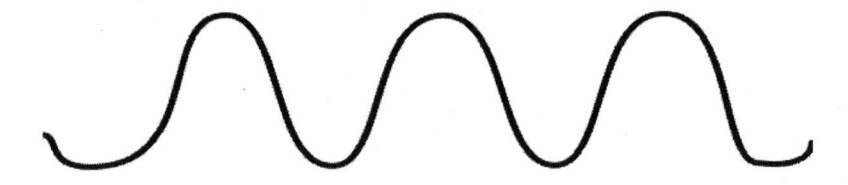

Lots of people have jobs that are similar to that drawing. People who are performers are always living like this. If they are getting ready for a play or a concert or maybe a show where they will display their art, or if they are making a movie, their lives really have ups and downs.

Do you have ups and downs in your life?

What contributes to your ups and downs?

Today is _____

Balance

If I want balance in my life, I will need to learn to do more than one thing at a time. If I think about a high-wire walker (a tightrope walker), I know that he has to move his arms, hands, legs, feet, and trunk. He is always moving one or more parts of his body in order to stay balanced.

I can learn to do the same thing in my life. I can move the different parts of it as I need to, so that I can have some balance. For example, even though I may really like to work, I know that it is also important for me to have friends and to eat well and to exercise. Even though I may like sports best, I also need to study, or work if I am old enough, and I also need to stay in touch with my friends. If I can do most of this most of the time, I can lead a pretty balanced life. This is the kind of life that I want. This is the kind of life that I will have.

Draw yourself on a tightrope.

Now, put names on the parts of your body that can stand for different things that you do. For example, your arms could be your friendships with others. Your legs could be your work or school life, and the trunk of your body could be your family. Your fingers could be exercise, and your feet could be the way you eat. Now, make up your own labels for your body parts and see how balanced you look.

Today is _____

OUT OF BALANCE

Even though I may really want a balanced life, a life in which I take very good care of myself, there may be times when things get a little out of balance. If I am going to have three tests in the next week, I probably need to study more than usual. If I am trying to shape up my body, I will probably want to exercise almost every day. But, if I find that I have a special need and am trying to keep everything in balance, I may be further stressing myself by trying to keep balanced. This is to miss the point.

The further I go in my recovery, the better I can take care of myself, and sometimes that means that for short times things will be a little unbalanced just because that is how they really need to be. When this happens I may feel uneasy, but I can tell myself that this is just how it is going to be for a while, and then I will stop fighting it and begin to relax.

When was the last time you felt out of balance?

What did you do about feeling out of balance?

Which way are you more comfortable?

How are you feeling right now?

Today is _____

Recovery Is A Process

Recovery is a process. There is a beginning, followed by many steps along the way. Each of the steps takes time. The process often begins when I know that something is wrong — that there is some kind of problem.

I may figure out that something is wrong in my family because I see or hear things from others that suggest a problem, or I may think something is wrong because someone tells me something that worries me, or I may look around and realize that my family members and I are playing roles. Any one of these things might happen to suggest to me that there is a problem. Any one of them may begin my process of recovery.

How did you first happen to think there was a problem in your family?

When did this process begin for you?

Today is _____

Recovery Is A Process

The process of recovery begins with an awareness that there is a problem. Once I become aware of a problem, I can begin to gather some information about it.

I can do this in different ways. I can find things to read that tell about some of the problems families have. A librarian can help me at my school or at a public library. I can talk to a counselor or teacher at school. I can talk to a friend or a family member, even a family member who is just a little bit apart from the family members I actually live with, such as an aunt, uncle, or grandparent. If I am in counseling, I can talk with my counselor. If I am in a group such as Alateen, I can talk in the group meetings or privately with the leader.

I can use any or all of these ways to get useful information about the problem in my family.

What do you think are the problems in your family?

What kind of information do you want to find out?

Where can you go to find out the information?

What kind of plans do you need to make in order to get to places where the information is available?

Today is _____

Recovery Is A Process

Once I have begun to gather information about a particular problem, what will I do with it? If I get my information through reading, I may want to find someone to talk with.

It might be hard for me to talk with someone about private things that are going on in my family, so I want to go only to people whom I really trust. The people I talk with might be a teacher, counselors, an Alateen leader, or other family members, or I might want to talk with a parent of one of my best friends. These are all people who know me well, and I should be able to trust them as I talk with them.

If you have gathered some information, what are you going to do with it?

Make a list of the people you really trust.

Who do you want to talk with first?

Today is _____

Recovery Is A Process

If I am from a family that has problems, I may have learned to cope in either of two ways. I may want to talk about my problems with everybody I see, or I may not want to talk about them with anyone at all.

As I move through the process of recovery, I can learn to trust people more. I can learn how to sort out who is going to keep quiet about what I tell them. I can find this out by telling someone just a little and then seeing what they do with it. In other words, does the person keep quiet about what I say? Does she or he seem to understand and respect me? Does that person take me seriously?

Who do you plan to talk with?

How will you give out your information so that you can see if you can really trust the person you are talking with?

Today is _____

Recovery Is A Process

I do not need to be in a hurry to change my behaviors. I can change them as I become comfortable changing them. I will be on this journey the rest of my life, and that is OK. It may take me the rest of my life to become the person I really want to be. I do not need to rush.

If I have been a Hero in my family, I might not like this suggestion. I may want myself and everyone around me to be different yesterday! With most families, it just does not work this way. In fact, since change is difficult for most people, I will expect it to take time. I will expect myself and others to slip back into old habits when stressful things come up, and when this happens, I will just pick myself up and get on with it again.

You have the rest of your life to change the behaviors that you want to change. Which behavior are you working on changing now?

Today is _____

Recovery Is A Process

A lot of people get to a point in their recovery where they are changing their behaviors. For some people this is a stopping point. They are really not interested in moving along further in their process of recovery.

Sometimes I think that this will be enough for me. Other times, I want to go further and really try to get rid of the painful feelings that are inside me, the ones that have been there since before I began to slip into a role in order to build a wall of defenses around myself.

How far do I want to go in my recovery?

Where do I think that I am now?

Where do I want to be?

Today is _____

Recovery Is A Process

Why would I want to go further? What will I gain by understanding the feelings that are inside me? As long as I keep such feelings as anger, sadness, fear, guilt, or loneliness inside me, it will be hard for me to let down my wall of defenses.

I want to remember that I built my wall of defenses in the first place in order to protect myself from the feelings inside me, to hide my pain. As long as the feelings are inside me, I may feel that I need my role, my defenses, to protect me, because while I am playing my role, I do not have to let my feelings out. It might still be too scary.

What are the feelings inside you?

Are there feelings inside you that frighten you?

Which feelings frighten you the most?

56

Today is 8/4/25

The Box

Here is something that might help me with making useful changes in my life. I can make a box with four squares like this:

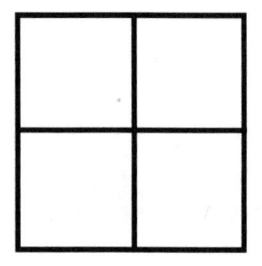

```
┌───┬───┐
│   │   │
├───┼───┤
│   │   │
└───┴───┘
```

Now, I can make a sort of timeline with the four squares. For example, I can label the top left square as "Right Now," the top right square as "Soon," the bottom left square as "A Lot Later," and the right bottom square as "Never in a Million Years." My labeled box will look something like this:

RIGHT NOW My anger towards others. My eating challenges. My temper. My outbursts	**SOON**
A LOT LATER	**NEVER IN A MILLION YEARS** My kindness, my loyalty, my sillyness, my softyness

Now, focus on the first box. Write in some behaviors that you want to change now. What are they?

Take some time to write things in the other three boxes, too.

Today is _____

THE BOX

An interesting thing is already happening with the box I filled in last week. Once I put things into each section, I became more willing to work on making those changes. This is even happening already with the things labeled, "Never in a Million Years." This is a really strange feeling for me — something that I surely did not expect! I wonder why this is happening.

You are experiencing what many others have experienced with the use of this kind of a box. Once something gets listed there, it is common for you to begin to work on it — at least in your mind. This may be happening with you already.

Draw a picture of your reaction to the changes you are feeling, now that you have completed all of the squares in your box.

Today is _____

The Funnel

Everyone is born with a natural range of feelings. All of us come into this world able to feel happy, sad, angry, afraid, guilty, and confused. If I watch a young baby, I can see that babies have no trouble experiencing and showing all their feelings. Yet as a small child grows, the people around that child sometimes put pressure on to keep the child from expressing its natural feelings. Grown-ups may tell the child, "You should not feel that way," but the child feels a certain way no matter what the adults may think. In some families it is not acceptable to express anger. In other families it is not acceptable to show fear.

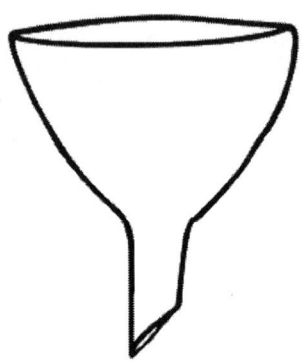

After a while, it seems that all the original feelings go into a big funnel, leaving only one feeling to come out. Some people almost always appear angry, or sad, or confused, or afraid. Some people even always appear happy, although deep down they are not really that way. Until they learn to behave differently, people who funnel their feelings ignore most of their natural feelings and express just those that their family will allow.

Is there one feeling you have more than any other?

Which feeling is that?

Do you think you have ever funneled your feelings?

What other feelings do you want to be able to express?

Can you draw a picture of your own funnel?

Today is _____

FEELINGS

As I decide to release the feelings inside me as well as change my behaviors, one feeling that may come up is sadness. Another feeling that may come up is anger. And, at times, I may feel OK. I will probably feel a mixture of sadness, anger, and OK.

As I start to let the feelings inside me out, I know that I will be grieving. Those feelings may come over me like big waves in an ocean. As those feelings want to come out, I may find myself getting very scared. I may want someone with me as I have these strong feelings. This might be a time to try to get into a support or therapy group, or look for a counselor who can give me suggestions for dealing with my feelings.

What are the feelings inside you?

Which feelings scare you now?

Today is _____

Feelings

Thinking and writing about feelings, I sometimes wonder if it might be possible just to stick with changing my behavior and forget about letting my feelings out. It sounds simpler and it sounds less scary. But as I wonder about this, I also doubt that it is really possible to change my behavior unless I let my feelings out.

After all, I slipped into the role that I have been playing in order to protect myself from painful feelings. Therefore, if I start to change my behavior and drop my role, my feelings may sort of automatically start to come out. This can be very confusing. Maybe this is one of those things I should not think about much but just start trying to do.

What feelings do you think your role has covered up?

How do you feel about letting those feelings out?

Today is _____

Denial

I want to move from denying things to dealing with them, but I'm wondering how to do it. Maybe starting to talk more honestly about what is going on will help me begin to move away from denying. I wonder whether starting to talk about things is a way I can begin to shed my role and start to move toward letting my feelings out. Maybe this is what I will begin to try.

Starting to talk about things seems much less scary than just beginning to let my feelings out. I can talk. If I talk first, then I may become more comfortable with my feelings. Talking is a good way to start shedding my role, and at the same time it will help me drop some of the behaviors that I have used as defenses.

What has happened in your family that you would like to talk about?

Who would you like to talk with?

Today is _____

Denial

As I think about talking about some of the things that have happened in my family, things I believe we have denied, I am beginning to feel a little frightened and excited at the same time. Some of the things may have happened a while ago, and so I feel a little strange bringing them up. Sometimes I wonder whether I can really remember them all myself. I also wonder whether other people will remember things differently from the way I recall them. I guess the only way I will get answers to my questions is to start talking about something and see what other people say.

How long ago did the thing you want to talk about happen?

What other members of your family knew about the event at the same time you did?

Who do you plan to talk with first?

Today is _____

Denial

I am wondering whether denial, fear, and honesty may somehow be related. I guess I am thinking that if people try to pretend that things that happened did not really happen, they are not really being honest. But I wonder whether they are not being honest because they are really afraid of the truth — maybe they are afraid to talk about hard things, things that may be painful to themselves or others.

As I think about my feelings, I realize I have some of these feelings, too. I have known for a good while that I have some fear of talking about things that happened in the past, and I worry a little about how honest other people will be when I bring such things up.

As you think back to something you believe your family has denied, what are you feeling?

Are you worried about people being honest?

Are you frightened?

Today is _____

Holidays

I am discovering that, as I talk with others, I can often find someone who really does understand what I am going through. By talking with others, I also learn that I am not alone with my feelings. I am finding that a lot of people out there look forward to holidays and other special times for some reasons but also dread them for other reasons. Before I started talking to others, I thought I was the only one who had these feelings. Now I know that this is just not how it is.

Who have you been talking to most?

What kinds of things have you been talking about?

How do you feel now that you have been talking?

Today is _____

LONELINESS

I am also learning that I can feel isolated even when I am with other people. In fact, sometimes I feel loneliest when I am in a crowd. Some of my loneliness comes from feeling that I am so different from other people that they will not understand me. The more I feel this way the more isolated and alone I feel. And, the more alone I feel, the more lonely and sad I can become.

I want to find ways to get out of my loneliness. I want to find ways to connect with other people. I know there must be others out there who have also had problems in their families.

When do you feel most alone?

What do you do when you feel lonely?

What other kinds of feelings do you have when you feel lonely?

Today is _____

LONELINESS

One of the reasons that I often feel lonely is that sometimes I am uneasy around other people. When I imagine that I am the only one in the world who has the problems I have, it is easy for me to think that I do not want to be around others, or that they would not want to be around me.

When I feel uneasy about being with other people, I sometimes want to stay by myself. I find that I can sometimes become afraid of other people. I worry about what they will think of me and whether I will feel more alone with them or by myself. Isolation can be a big problem for me, a problem that is sometimes related to being uneasy around other people.

Has there ever been a time when you were uneasy about being around other people?

Draw a picture of the situation in which you felt uneasy about being around others.

What did you do when you felt uneasy about being around other people?

Today is _____

Uneasiness

When I am uneasy about being around others, I may behave in various ways. I can be very quiet. I can talk all the time. I can clown around and act as if whatever is happening is really funny. I can "put down" what is going on and talk about it as if it is really stupid. Or I can try to relax and take in what is happening, once I know that I really do not have to do very much.

It helps me to relax when I remember that everyone else who is there may feel just as uneasy about being there as I do. I can learn not to judge a person's insides by their outsides. In other words, I cannot look at the way someone is acting and then know how that person really feels. As I relax, I may find that I am less uneasy.

How do you feel when you are around people you do not know very well?

How do you act when you are around people you do not know very well?

Draw a picture of what you might do to relax when you are feeling uneasy.

Today is _____

Dealing with Criticism

One thing I have noticed about myself is that if someone criticizes me, I often feel threatened. I may feel as if the critical statement is somehow really true of me, and these feelings may make me feel scared. Criticism may often scare me. It may scare me a lot. I may react by thinking that people do not like me, or that they are talking about me behind my back, or that I need to think up ways to make them like me.

I want to change this about myself. I want to learn to react differently to criticism. I want to learn to be less threatened, because, after all, people who are the most critical of me often have a lot of their own problems. In fact, they may be criticizing me because of the way they feel about themselves.

Are there people in your life who criticize you a lot? If so, who?

How do you feel when people criticize you?

What do you do when people criticize you?

Today is _____

Dealing with Criticism

One of the tricks to learning to deal with criticism is becoming able to really think carefully about what people are saying. I do not want to assume automatically just because someone says something about me that it is true, but neither do I want to think automatically that what they said is not true.

I want to learn to be able to take criticism in, to think about whether any of it fits me or not, and then decide what to do about it. By doing this I can also understand something of what is going on with the person who criticizes me. I can learn to deal with criticism so that it does not threaten me.

How have you been dealing with criticism?

How do you want to learn to deal with criticism?

How does criticism threaten you?

Today is _____

Family Problems

As I have been looking at my problems and those of my family, I have also been starting to think about some other families I know. I am realizing that all the families I know well have some kind of problem. The kinds of problems they have may be different from the problems we have in my family, but they all have problems of some kind.

Some families have trouble getting good jobs. In other families that have a lot of money, people are always angry and upset with each other over their money. Some families include people who drink too much. Some people have family members who take drugs, either the kind that they buy on the street or too many of what their doctors prescribe. Other families include someone who gambles or works too much, and a few families include a person who is very ill and needs a lot of care.

As I get to know more and more people, I see how many kinds of problems people can have.

What kinds of problems have you seen in the families you know best?

What kinds of problems do you think your family has?

How do you feel when you think about your family's problems?

Today is _____

Responsibility

Sometimes I have what can be called an "overdeveloped sense of responsibility." This means that I often try to take responsibility for everything that happens around me. If I hear a car crash down the block, I imagine there might have been something I could have done to stop it. If a friend of mine has a problem, I may think I should be able to solve it. I can get myself very confused thinking about all kinds of things that have happened and what I see as my responsibility for them.

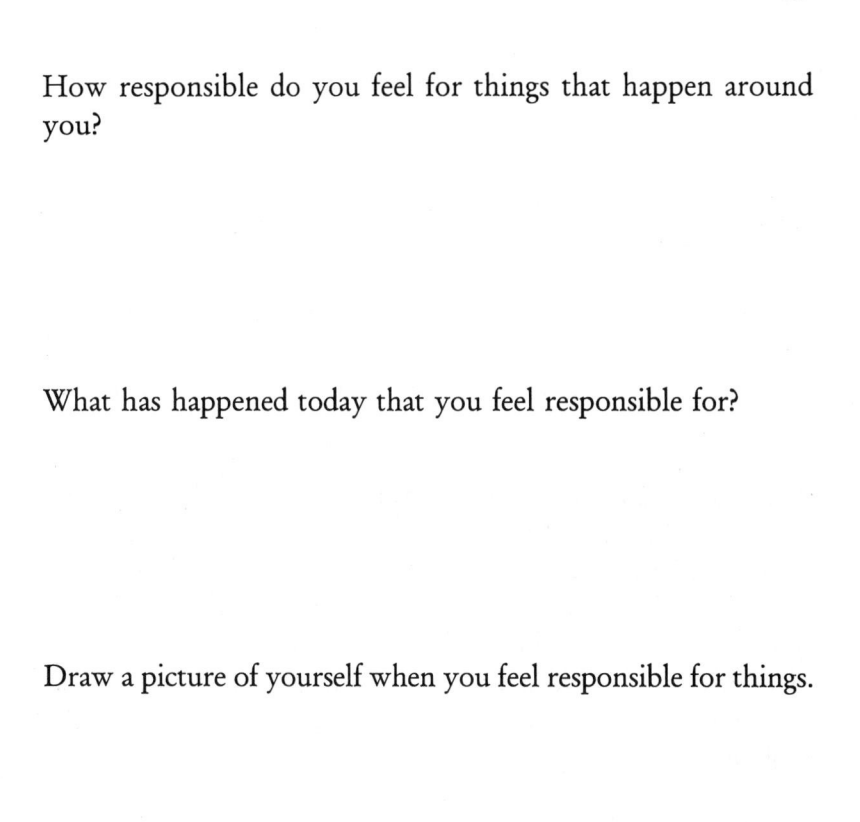

How responsible do you feel for things that happen around you?

What has happened today that you feel responsible for?

Draw a picture of yourself when you feel responsible for things.

Today is _____

Enabling

When someone close to me behaves in destructive ways, I just want it to stop. Yet however much I may want this behavior to stop, I am gradually learning that I cannot control what another person does.

Well-meaning family members and friends often do things that actually allow another person to stay stuck in destructive behavior. They may hide someone's mistakes, make excuses, or tell lies to keep that person from having hurt feelings or getting deeper into difficulty. Or they may provide for the person's compulsive behavior to continue, so that the compulsive person will not get angry at them. This is called "enabling."

Maybe it would be good for me to think whether I might even be doing something myself that allows another person to continue in destructive behavior. If I do any of those things, maybe I am an enabler myself sometimes.

Think of a family member who does something he or she cannot stop — something compulsive. Now think about what other family members do when that person is acting compulsively. Are the family members doing things that actually permit the person to continue in the behavior? Jot something down for several family members here.

Today is _____

ENABLING

When I consider enabling, I have trouble imagining why anyone would do something to help another person stay stuck in harmful behavior. Perhaps they believe they are helping by keeping the person from getting into deeper trouble. Or perhaps the enabling person gets good feelings from trying to "help," so the person they care about won't experience painful consequences.

I do know that people learn from experience. And so I can see that whenever the enabler steps in to relieve someone else from being responsible for his or her own actions, the enabler is stopping the irresponsible one from learning lessons that need to be learned.

If a wife keeps beer in the refrigerator even though her husband is an alcoholic, she is enabling her husband's drinking. If a Mom and Dad let their son drive even though they know he also drinks, they are enabling his drinking and driving. If a Grandma keeps the cookie jar full even though one of her granddaughters is overweight, that Grandma is enabling her granddaughter's overeating. These are just a few of the ways family members enable behaviors in others.

Can you write about examples of enabling you have seen?

Can you reflect upon times when you acted to keep someone from experiencing painful consequences? List or draw those things.

What might you do differently if it came up again?

Today is _____

Concern for Others

One characteristic of people from families that have a lot of problems is that they often show a great deal of concern for others. Concern for others is important, and no one is saying that we all should not be concerned for others, but sometimes I am so concerned with others that I become totally focused on them and their stuff.

Sometimes I can even describe myself as being "obsessed" with the problems of others. When I am doing this, I am not able to focus on my own stuff. I am not doing what I need to do to take care of myself.

Do you often find yourself feeling a lot of concern for others?

Who have you been most concerned about recently?

What have you missed out on for yourself while you have been concerned about that person?

Where should your focus be?

Today is _____

LOVE OR PITY?

If I grew up in a family that had a lot of problems, I may be confused about love and pity. For example, I may feel sorry for people, and then, as I feel sorry for them, I may come to feel that I love them.

Sometimes it may be hard for me to know the difference between feeling sorry for someone and loving them. If I see someone who needs something, I may be immediately drawn to that person. I may want to help them. I may want to get to know them — to get close to them. As I do this, I may feel that I love them, but my feelings really may have started out as pity for them. Have I ever confused pity and love?

Is there someone you have pitied?

Do you feel you have grown to love that person?

Do you think that you have confused love and pity?

If so, how does that confusion look?

Today is _____

Rescuing

Another part of confusing love and pity is that we may be attracted to people we pity because we may want to rescue them. We may want to try to save them. In other words, when we meet someone who has a problem, we may want to be their friend because we want to save them from their problem. We may believe that if we become friends with that person, we will be able to change them. We may believe that, by getting to know us, they will be able to leave their problems behind and become happier and healthier.

This is especially true if there were serious problems in the family in which we grew up. If someone in our family gambled a lot, for example, we might also be attracted to a gambler, and we might think that if the gambler gets to know us he or she will stop gambling and lead a "better" life. This almost never happens. Lots of people are attracted to gamblers or drinkers thinking that they will change, but it is sad to say that people seldom change just because they have met someone new.

Have you ever tried to rescue someone?

What happened when you tried to rescue them?

How do you feel about rescuing someone now?

Today is _____

Rescuing

Sometimes people think that if they rescue others and show them or give them "a better life," the other person will immediately be attracted to it. The rescuer may think that is all they have to do — show the other person the way. It seldom works like that.

Unfortunately, most people decide to change only if and when they are in a lot of pain, and this pain often has to be of their own making. In other words, if a person drinks too much, she or he may not stop drinking until after they lose their friends, job, home, health, driver's license, or other things that are really important to them. Such persons seldom change just because someone around them shows them it is possible to live without drinking.

Have you known people who have gone through many changes?

What do you think those persons have changed?

Today is _____

Excitement

People who grew up in troubled families often learn to have constant upsets in their lives. One person said, "It is as if every issue is a crisis."

People who live like this usually experience a lot of chaos. When something happens that in the grand scheme of things would be considered rather minor, the person makes a REALLY BIG DEAL out of it. Some might describe this as "making a mountain out of a molehill." Something fairly little happens (like having a flat tire, for example), but the person acts as if the world is coming to an end. After all, having a flat tire is usually aggravating, but in the grand scheme of things it is not really such a big deal.

What was the last thing you got really worked up about?

In the grand scheme of things, how important was that thing?

Do you think you may be inclined to make mountains out of molehills?

Today is _____

Mountains and Molehills

My last reading included the phrase "making mountains out of molehills." I want to think about that for a bit.

I can picture a mountain, even if I have not really seen a mountain. I know they can be very high — so high that it is not possible to see the top from the ground if I am looking straight up. Some mountains are so high that their tops are always in the clouds.

A molehill, on the other hand, is really small. Moles are no bigger than mice, so the hills they make are just little rises in the earth. They are probably no higher than an inch or so.

So if I am making a mountain out of a molehill, I am really talking about turning something little into something REALLLLLLLLLLY big. If I have a tendency to do that, I might want to think about whether I could be addicted to excitement.

I may thrive on excitement. I may want life to be as exciting as possible because that excitement can give me a real rush. This can be the same kind of feeling that someone else gets from using drugs or alcohol or gambling! I am going to check out my needs for excitement.

Do you often make mountains out of molehills?

What was the last mountain that you made out of a molehill?

What did it feel like for you to make a mountain out of a molehill?

Is it possible that you are addicted to excitement?

Today is _____

Excitement

If I am a person who is addicted to excitement, I may not even make time to look for signs of a change in the seasons. I may be too busy carrying on about whatever has happened to me most recently even to notice what is happening in the world around me.

On the other hand, if I can slow myself down long enough to look at the world around me, this can be a step toward getting away from being addicted to excitement. I can begin to let go of being focused upon little stuff. I can begin to notice things without needing to get carried away with excitement about them. I can take time to look, and see, and be.

Do you think you are or have ever been addicted to excitement?

How has this addiction shown itself?

What happens when you begin to slow down?

What do you want to do with yourself today?

Today is _____

HOLIDAYS

Everyone wants to think of holidays as happy times. For many people, though, holidays can be very painful. In some families, people drink too much or take drugs at holiday times, and there is unhappiness and unpleasantness as a result. When families are split up, or in a state of conflict, holidays can add to people's pain.

If I go into holidays expecting that they will be wonderful, then if things turn out not so wonderful, I may be sad, let down, or depressed.

Because I am a strong person, before a holiday comes, I can make choices about what I will say, think, and do. I can plan how I will handle my feelings — talk to someone I trust, plan activities to fill the time, create a holiday tradition all my own. I can make my own plans, and that feels good. And if my family's observances are not what I hoped for, I can learn to detach myself from whatever happens without feeling that it was my fault, or that I was helpless to change things.

What new ideas do you have for spending holiday times?

Can you write or draw about these ideas?

What do you have to do in order to follow through with your plans?

Who can help you make it happen?

Today is _____

A Higher Power

One solution for my problems is a really simple one, yet it is one some people have a lot of trouble with. I know now that when something happens, I am not alone. My Higher Power is always with me, and if I want to, there are people around that I can talk to, and people I can call up and talk with on the telephone.

Yes, the telephone is one of my solutions today. One girl told me that her father used to say, "Just pick up the phone...." This was a Dad who knew that his kids might want to talk to him when things happened. He was very wise to use this simple sentence, "Just pick up the phone...." as his kids grew up. By the time they got old enough to leave home, they had heard him say "Just pick up the phone...." so many times that when things happened to them it just came naturally — they picked up the phone.

That Dad made himself available to his kids even when they no longer lived in the same town. I know that I have people around me that I can talk to when I want to or need to, if I "just pick up the phone."

How often do you use the telephone?

Who do you like to call when you really have something on your mind?

If you do not already "just pick up the phone," make a list here of people you could call when something happens.

How does it feel to you to call someone when you are upset?

Today is _____

God Box

One of the ways I can learn to stop obsessing about a problem of mine is to make a box that I call my "God Box" or "Higher Power Box" or some other name that fits how I plan to use it.

It can be a big box or a small box. It can be fancy with pretty paper all over it, or it can be plain. The most important thing about this box is that I make it in such a way that I can put little pieces of paper into it and then not be able to get them out!

The whole point is that when I write down something that is bothering me on a piece of paper and stick that piece of paper into the box, I am turning the problem over to my Higher Power. Once I do this, I want to leave that issue with my Higher Power.

What kind of box do you want to make?

What has been happening in your life that you might want to turn over?

Do you have time today to put together a box?

Do you have little pieces of paper that you can keep with your box, so that it is ready for you to use whenever you feel like it?

Today is _____

The Same Box

Last week I learned how to make a box that I can put pieces of paper into when things are bugging me. I may even have made a box for myself by now. If I did not get one made last week, I may have time today.

When something is really bugging me I know that I think about it many times a day. If this happens, I can write down a word or phrase that describes the issue and stick it into the box.

For example, if my parents are having a rough time and I am worried about their marriage, I might write down, "Mom and Dad's marriage" on a little piece of paper and stick it into the box. If I first thought about their marital problems when I got up this morning, I can write it down and stick it into my box. If I think about it again right after breakfast, I can put another piece of paper in then. If I think of it again about noon, in goes another piece of paper, and so on through the day.

Every time my problem comes back to me, I can turn it over again. If I am really going to do this, maybe I need to make a BIG box.

Use a little time today to make a box if you feel like it, and make some little strips of paper to stick in it.

If you have already made your box and begun putting your problems inside, write a little about how that feels to you.

Today is _____

A Higher Power

I am noticing that if I can put my trust in a Higher Power, I feel calmer. It makes a difference for me to know that there is a power greater than myself. Instead of making me feel small and little and less-than, my Higher Power fills me with peace because I can let go of some things. I know that some things just are not under my control.

The things that I turn over to my Higher Power can stay with my Higher Power. I can really "turn them over." I do not have to force answers. I can relax more and know that things will work out the way they are supposed to. And even though I may not like the way they work out, I can learn to accept them.

Sometimes I can even look back after something happens and see that even though I was really upset about it when it happened, it was something that has made a good difference in my life. This is especially true if I have learned to turn some things over to my Higher Power.

Draw a picture of how your Higher Power looks to you.

Is there something in your life you can look back on and see now how it fits into the whole picture?

What is that thing that happened some time ago?

How do you feel about it now?

Today is _____

RECOGNIZING LOVE

If I have grown up with people who do not know what love really is, or people who lack healthy ways of showing their love, I may have difficulty recognizing healthy love. How can I tell whether someone truly loves me?

A person who truly loves me treats me with respect. That person recognizes that I have my own ideas, that I am separate from them, and that is OK. A person who truly loves me tries to understand me even when they do not agree with me.

A person who loves me can empathize with my feelings. That person knows that when I say I am upset about something, I am upset. They do not try to talk me out of my feelings by changing my mind about things.

A person who loves me never tries to impose their will on mine, never manipulates me to get their way. They are always kind to me. A person who truly loves me values me and knows how to cherish me.

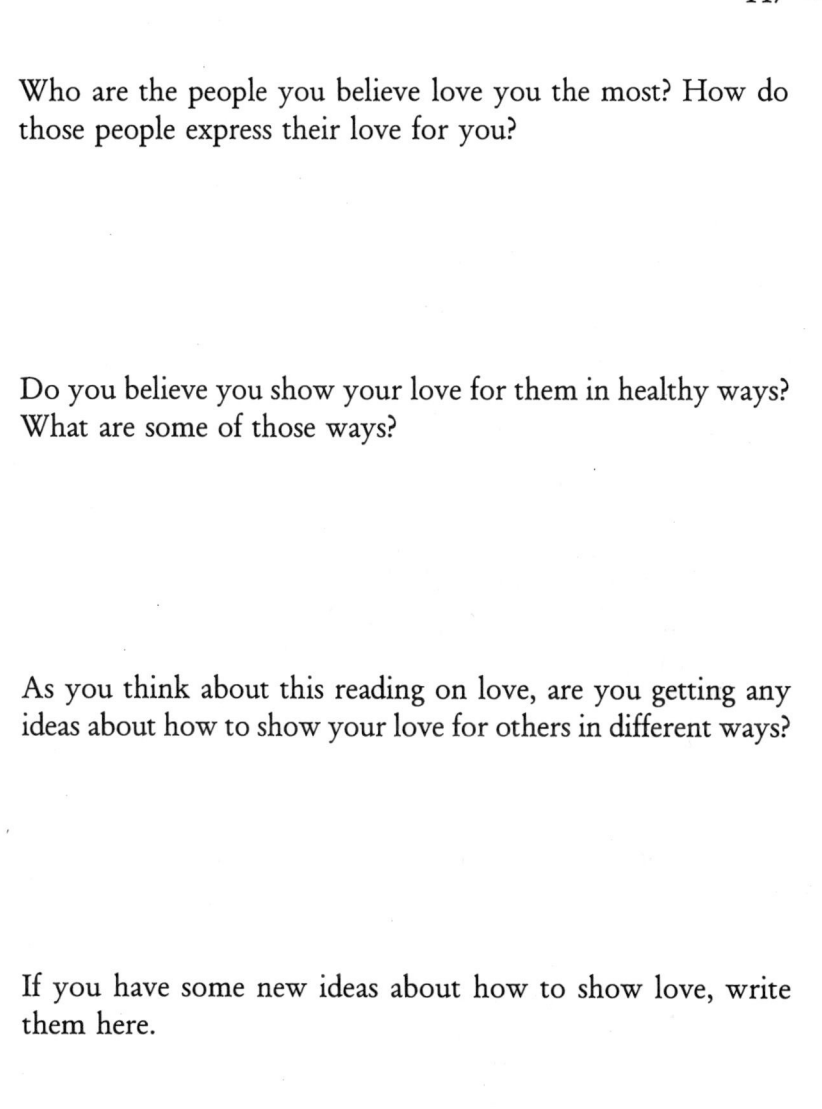

Who are the people you believe love you the most? How do those people express their love for you?

Do you believe you show your love for them in healthy ways? What are some of those ways?

As you think about this reading on love, are you getting any ideas about how to show your love for others in different ways?

If you have some new ideas about how to show love, write them here.

Today is _____

My Birthday

There is an old saying
that before a baby is born
God kisses its soul
and that
as its guardian angel
bears it to its little body
    She sings
    Is there in my subconscious self
    still a dim memory of that kiss,
    a faint echo of that song?

Is there in your subconscious self still a dim memory of that kiss?

Is there a faint echo of that song?

Draw a picture of yourself as the baby that heard the song and felt the kiss.

120

Now that you have done all of the readings and exercises, draw another picture of yourself here.

How different are your pictures? How much have you changed?

INDEX

Anger 62
Attention — getting & not getting 24-29
Baby 60, 118-119
Balance 38-41
Birthday 118-119
Box, The 56-59
Box, God 110-113
Calming down 14-15
Changing behaviors 50-67, 96-99
Choices 6-7
Clown 24-25
Compulsive behavior 88-89
Concern for others 92-93
Counseling 62
Criticism 80-83
Defenses 10, 22-27, 32, 52-54
Denial 32-35, 66-71
Enabling 88-91, 96-97
Excitement 100-105
Families 10-11
Family problems 10-11, 84-85
Family systems 10-11
Fear 54-55, 70-71
Feeling different 72-75
Feelings 10-13, 22, 32-37, 52-55, 60-67, 70-73
Funnel, The 60-61
God Box 110-113
Healthy families 10
Higher Power 108-111, 114-115
Holidays 72-73, 106-107
Honesty 70-71
Isolation 74-76
Loneliness 74-76
Love 94-96, 116-117
Love & pity 94-97
Mountains & molehills 100-103

Obsession with others   92-93
Pacing myself   36-37
Painful consequences   90-91, 98-99
Pity   94-97
Problems
  Awareness of   44-45
  Coping with   48
  Family   84-85
  Information about   44-47
  Solving   14-15
  Talking about   10-11, 46-49, 66-69
  Turning over   110-115
  Types of   84-85
Recovery process   42-55
Rescuing   88-91, 96-98
Responsibility   86-87
Roles   10-11, 16-35, 52-55, 64-65
  Hero   16-27, 31, 50-51
  Lonely/Lost Child   28-29, 31
  Mascot   24-27, 30-31
  Scapegoat/Troublemaker   20-27, 30-31
Sadness   62, 74
Self-care   8-9, 12-13, 36, 92-93
Support group   62
Telephone   108-109
Therapy   62
Thinking   14-15
Trust   46-49, 114
Trying to help   90-91, 94
Uneasiness   76-79
Ups and downs   36-37

Forthcoming Books by Linda Meyer

Recovery 101: A Meditation Journal for Teens and the Young at Heart. 366 entries and exercises for people from troubled families.

Eldercare: A Family's Greatest Challenge. This book chronicles a family's care of an elderly woman from the time of her diagnosis as an alcoholic until her death, while raising important questions for families with similar problems and making recommendations that have already proven helpful to many other families.

I Can Look at Me. A colorbook for children ages 3-10. Each page contains a sentence or more that can stimulate recovery and a line drawing for children to color or a box for children to draw in. Most effective when a parent or other adult works with a child.

Talks & Workshops Led by Linda Meyer

Programs offered:

- Strategies for helping children from troubled families to recover
- Exercises for the young at heart
- Working with adolescents

Each of these workshops will focus on practical help for families, counselors, and other helping professionals who work with children and adolescents.

For information, call

(217) 367-8821

or write to Linda Meyer
403 South Wright Street
Champaign, Illinois 61820

Do you
"have a book in you"

?

Recovery
Communications, Inc.
BOOK PUBLISHER
is looking for authors with interesting
book ideas, in a variety of topics:

Creativity **Relationships**
BUSINESS *Spirituality* Healing
The Joy of Living etc. etc.

We're open to new ideas!!
Contact us about our cooperative
publishing program.

**Call Betsy Tice White
Acquisitions Editor**

(770) 590-7311

More Books from Recovery Communications, INC.

Books available through your local bookstore

> — *and* —
> all authors are available for speaking
> and consulting nationwide

Diary of Abuse/Diary of Healing
by Jennifer J. Richardson, M.S.W.
Secret journal of a child, from age 6 til adulthood, recording two decades of physical and sexual abuse, with detailed healing therapy sessions. A very raw and extraordinary book.
Contact the author to speak at: (404) 373-1837

Turning Your Teen Around
How A Couple Helped Their Troubled Son
While Keeping Their Marriage Alive and Well
by Betsy Tice White
A doctor family's successful personal battle against teen-age drug use, with dozens of *powerfully* helpful tips for parents in pain. Describes the full gamut of emotions and healing of the entire family. Endorsed by John Palmer, NBC News.
Contact the author to speak at: (770) 590-7311

Getting Them Sober, Volume One
by Toby Rice Drews
Hundreds of ideas for sobriety and recovery. Endorsed by "Dear Abby" and Dr. Norman Vincent Peale.
Contact the author to speak at: (410) 243-8352

Getting Them Sober, Volume Four
Separation Decisions
by Toby Rice Drews
If you feel depressed because you can't leave; if you've left and gone back; much more.
Contact the author to speak at: (410) 243-8352

Mountain Folk, Mountain Food
Down-Home Wisdom, Plain Tales, and Recipe Secrets from Appalachia
by Betsy Tice White
The joy of living as expressed in charming vignettes and mouth-watering regional foods! Endorsed by the TV host of "Great Country Inns" and by *Blue Ridge Magazine*.
Contact the author to speak at: (770) 590-7311

Wise Stuff About Relationships
by Joseph L. Buccilli, Ph.D.
A *gem* of a book; "an empowering spiritual workout." Endorsed by the vice president of the *Philadelphia Inquirer*.
Contact the author to speak at: (609) 629-4441

Eastern Shore Beckonings
by John Pearson
Marvelous trek back in time through charming villages and encounters with solid Chesapeake Bay folks.
Contact the author to speak at: (410) 315-7940